MW01122631

The Ginger Princess

THE GINGER PRINCESS

by

William Pasnak

James Lorimer & Company Ltd., Publishers
Toronto

© 1988, 2006 William Pasnak

All rights reserved. No part of this book may be reproduced or transmitted in any form or by any means, electronic or mechanical, including photocopying, or by any information storage or retrieval system, without permission in writing from the publisher.

James Lorimer & Company Ltd. acknowledges the support of the Ontario Arts Council. We acknowledge the support of the Government of Canada through the Book Publishing Industry Development Program (BPIDP) for our publishing activities. We acknowledge the support of the Canada Council for the Arts for our publishing program. We acknowledge the support of the Government of Ontario through the Ontario Media Development Corporation's Ontario Book Initiative.

Series cover design: Iris Glaser Canada Council   Conseil des Arts
for the Arts   du Canada

Library and Archives Canada Cataloguing in Publication

Pasnak, William, 1949-
[Mimi and the ginger princess]
    The ginger princess / William Pasnak.
(Streetlights)
First published in 1988 under title: Mimi and the ginger princess.
ISBN-13: 978-1-55028-952-7
ISBN-10: 1-55028-952-7
    I. Title. II. Title: Mimi and the ginger princess. III. Series.
PS8581.A7675M6 2006   jC813'.54   C2006-903624-1

James Lorimer & Company Ltd., Publishers   Distributed in the
317 Adelaide Street West   United States by:
Suite 1002   Orca Book Publishers
Toronto, Ontario, M5V 1P9   P.O. Box 468
www.lorimer.ca   Custer, WA USA
                                              98240-0468

Printed and bound in Canada.

1

MIMI SANK DOWN on her heels in the back alley and made a hissing, whispering noise through her lips. *Psss-pss-pss-pss.* It was a quick little sound, like the paws of a mouse running across dry leaves. *Psss-pss-pss-pss.*

Mimi knew there was a kitten behind the Rutledges' garbage can. She had seen it slip into hiding when she turned down the alley. She knew it would come out again in a moment because no cat yet had been able to resist her cat-calling noise. Mimi knew every cat in the neighbour-hood, from Mr. Breland's fat little tabby, Ribbons, to the nameless black-and-white tom that lived under the bridge on Rat Creek.

Mimi was nine. She was short, with black hair that she wore in bangs. She could skip better than just about anyone in her class, except for her friend Paulette Nadeau, who had once got up to one hundred in double-pepper. When Mimi wrote her name, she did it in smooth round letters, with a beautiful curl that wrapped like a cat's tail into a dot over the *i* at the end of her name:

Kiguchi

like that.

Mimi could also make friends with any cat that was ever born. Once again she made the whistling whisper, and waited.

She thought the cat would peek around the side of the garbage can, but it fooled her. It jumped up on top of the can and crouched on the lid, staring at her with yellow eyes that were about as big as the headlights on a car. Mimi fell in love completely and immediately.

The cat was sleek, short-haired, sandy-ginger and beautiful snow-white, with a long skinny neck and hips that swung around as if they were on springs. Mimi knew instantly that the kitten was a girl. She could tell that she was only half grown, still full of electric kitten curiosity.

"Are you new here? Who do you belong to? I've never seen you before," Mimi said, making her voice soft and inviting. If the cat was a stray, maybe Mimi could talk her mum into letting her keep it. They had never had a cat before, but this one needed a home.

She made her noise again and gently rubbed her finger and thumb together. The cat gave her a quick look of interest. Then she began to survey a route to Mimi from the top of the can. Mimi knew she would leap down and come to her in just a second.

Then, without warning, Mimi was deafened by a loud yell. A dark shape shot over the top of the Rutledges' fence.

"There she is! We got her cornered!"

Ricky Rutledge landed heavily in the alley between Mimi and the cat. He was holding an enormous canvas mail bag. Slowly, Ricky straightened up, keeping his eye on the cat.

When Ricky had first yelled, the cat pulled herself in tight, as though someone had thrown ice water on her. Now she was standing with her four paws under her, staring at Ricky, ready to take off in any direction.

Ricky carefully lifted the mail bag and opened the mouth wide. Then he threw himself at the can, bringing the canvas bag down with a whoosh.

But the cat wasn't there.

The second Ricky launched himself at her, she shot to the top of the fence and took off. By the time Ricky was bouncing off the can and the fence with a heavy "Ooi," she had reached the corner of the Rutledges' yard. As Ricky and the garbage can fell over into the alley with a clatter, she jumped down into Mr. Neilsen's garden and disappeared.

Red with anger, Ricky jumped to his feet. He snatched up a rock the size of a plum and fired it after the cat. Mimi caught her breath, but the cat had already disappeared. The rock bounced harmlessly off Mr. Neilsen's garage with a loud *thwack*!

Looking down at himself, Ricky found he was covered with old coffee grounds, soggy paper towels, and eggshells.

"Oh, yuck!" he said. "Hot fudge yuck with onions!"

"It serves you right!" Mimi said hotly. "What did you want to scare her for?"

Ricky looked at Mimi as if he was seeing her for the first time. He was about twice as big as Mimi because he was two grades ahead of her in school. His belly hung over his belt, and his messy brown hair stuck out in all directions. He had small, unfriendly blue eyes and a little snub nose.

Mimi knew Ricky had a reputation for being mean to anyone smaller than himself. She backed away from him a bit, just in case she had to run for it.

"I didn't want to scare her," Ricky said. "I wanted to catch her."

"Well, you'll never catch her now," Mimi said. "You scared her so much her hair stood on end all the way to the end of her tail. When you do that

9

to a cat, she'll never come near you again in a skillion years. And," she added boldly, "I'm glad!"

Ricky's face turned even nastier, and Mimi suddenly thought she might have said too much.

"Oh, yeah?" he said. He leaned over to push his face close to hers. "We'll catch her, all right. We've got a team working on it. And when we do, we're going to use her for an experiment." He laughed meanly. "We might even let you watch, if you're good!"

Just then there was a scuffling noise. A strange combination of red hair, blue rubber, and glass appeared above the fence.

"H'wal clr my ma hmpoh hp ca'm," it said.

"Tim," Ricky said, "take that snorkel out of your mouth, will you? You sound like Gargo the Sloth Man."

Mimi saw now that it was red-haired Tim Flanagan, wearing a diver's mask and snorkel. Tim was as skinny as Ricky was fat. His cheekbones pushed out hard under his freckly skin.

Tim slipped the snorkel out of his mouth. "All clear by the compost heap, captain," he said again.

"I told you she wouldn't be there," Ricky said. "Didn't you hear me yell? I had her cornered out here, but she got away."

Tim peered through the faceplate at the mess around Ricky. "If you had her cornered, how come she got away?" he asked. "And how come you're covered with garbage?"

Before Ricky could answer, there was the sound of scrunching gravel, and the Rutledge station wagon turned into the alley. Mrs. Rutledge was at the wheel. She pulled up beside her son, rolled down the window and looked at him. Mimi saw that there was still some orange peel sitting on his running shoe.

"Hi, Mum," Ricky said, smiling brightly.

"I don't know what you have been doing," his mother said, "and I'm not sure I want to know. But I want that garbage, and I mean every scrap of it, picked up by the time I get the car in the garage, or there's going to be Big Trouble." She rolled the window up, then rolled it down again. "And if you've let Tim use your brother's mask and snorkel without asking him, you can forget

11

about your next birthday. He won't let you live that long."

Ricky's brother, Mark, was a cadet who wanted to be a weather man for the air force some day. Ricky was always "borrowing" his stuff.

Mrs. Rutledge rolled the car window up again, pushed the garage door opener, and put the car in gear. Ricky quickly began to scoop garbage back into the can, and Mimi decided it was a good time to be going.

As she walked away down the alley, she looked hopefully around for any sign of the beautiful little cat. She had disappeared completely, though. All Mimi could see was a black mark on the wall of Mr. Neilsen's garage, from the rock Ricky had thrown.

2

GRANDFATHER TAKEDA LIVED with Mimi's family. He was short and skinny, and he had soft, kind eyes. His silver-white hair was always brushed back so that it made Mimi think of a lion's mane. He called Mimi "Mi-chan," or sometimes "Midori," which was her real name. When she came in, he was sitting at the kitchen table, reading the newspaper to his friend, Mr. Uemura.

"Mi-chan," he said, "*okae-ri*. Welcome home."

"Hi, Grampa," Mimi said. "Hi, Mr. Uemura."

Mr. Uemura gave her the ghost of a smile and nodded about half a centimetre. He didn't say anything, though. He almost never spoke, and when he did, it was usually in a whisper nobody but Grampa could hear.

Mimi knew that Mr. Uemura always felt sad. His wife had died about a year before, so he was lonely. He couldn't see very well anymore, either. He wore thick glasses tinted a sort of yellowish-brown, but they didn't help much. That was why Grampa Takeda read the paper to him every day.

"How's the news?" Mimi asked.

"Mixed," her grandfather said. "So-so. The Blue Jays won a double-header, but the Yomiuri Giants lost."

"That's too bad. Isn't Mum home yet?"

"Not yet. She had to stay and pack carnations."

Mimi's mother worked for a big greenhouse out at the edge of town.

Because her mum wasn't home, Mimi knew she couldn't go and play with Paulette. She would have to stay and keep an eye on her little brother, Kenny, because soon Grampa Takeda would walk Mr. Uemura back to his house.

"Can I have a cookie?" she asked.

"Sure. Take one to Kenny, too. He's watching TV."

Kenny was three years old. He *might* be watching TV, Mimi thought, but he was probably getting in trouble. He was *always* getting in trouble.

Mimi got out the cookie tin with the pink and blue flowers on it. She pulled the lid off. Inside there was a pile of big, soft molasses cookies all stuck together, each one the size of her hand. She peeled off two of these, put them on a plate, and put the tin away. Then she poured two glasses of milk and tore off a square of paper towel because Kenny always spilled his a little.

Finally, she picked up the glasses with the plate balanced on top of one of them, and headed very carefully for the TV room.

The TV was on, but Kenny wasn't watching it. He was halfway to the ceiling on a pile of encyclopedias, trying to reach Hector, the stuffed owl perched on top of the bookshelf.

The pile of books was swaying dangerously as Kenny reached up toward the bird.

Carefully, Mimi set the plate and glasses on a table. "Kenny, come on down and have a cookie."

Kenny looked down at her with his bright, black eyes.

"Hectoh," he said stubbornly. He was, in fact, one of the most stubborn kids Mimi had ever met, and one of the roundest. Paulette said he was like a round rubber ball with a brush cut.

"Cookie," Mimi said. She pointed to the plate.

For a long moment Kenny stared at the plate. Then he turned back toward Hector.

"Okay," Mimi said. "I'll eat them both myself, then."

"No!" Kenny said, jerking around. "My cookie!"

It was the sudden move Mimi had been hoping to avoid. The stack of books slid out from under him like snow falling off the roof, sending Kenny crashing to the floor. For a second, the air was full of arms, legs and flying books. Then Kenny bounced up and grabbed both cookies from the plate.

"Just one," Mimi said, prying his little fingers open, "and then you have to help me pick up all the books and put them away."

Fortunately, the noise of the television had covered up the crash of the books and Kenny falling. Now, as Mimi turned the sound down, she heard something on the Junior Gopher Bulletin Board.

"... Science Fair," the voice was saying. "The best experiment will win a prize. For details — "

"Experiment!" Mimi said. "I wonder if that's what Ricky Rutledge was talking about. I bet he wants to do something mean to that cat for the Science Fair!"

She couldn't get the pretty little cat out of her mind. She could see her now, crouched on top of the garbage can ...

Just as she was finishing putting away the encyclopedias, Mimi heard the back door open, and her mother's voice in the kitchen. Mimi shoved the last book on the shelf upside down. She ran out to the kitchen, followed closely by Kenny.

"Hi, Mum," she said. "Can I go play with Paulette?"

"Yes," her mother said, giving them each a kiss. Mimi could smell the spicy carnation smell still clinging to her clothes. "But you'll have to take Kenny with you."

"But — "

"I'm not staying," her mother said. "I have to take the flowers to the airport. So you have to look after Kenny. But you can go and play with Paulette if you want to."

"Okay," Mimi said, trying not to sound too disappointed. Then she brightened. "Mum, can we have a kitten? She's really pretty, with white stockings and a sandy patch that runs right down onto her nose, and I don't think she belongs to anyone."

"You found a stray, did you? I'm sorry, Mimi, but we just can't. Your father's allergic to them."

"Well, he wouldn't have to play with her. I could do that."

"It doesn't matter if he plays with her or not, Mimi. If a cat just comes in the house, he gets all stuffed up and he can't breathe. You wouldn't want that to happen, would you?"

"Well, no ... I guess not. But he isn't home all the time. Would it really matter?" Mimi's father travelled a lot on business. In fact, he was away now, all the way up in Yellowknife.

Her mother gave her a look that Mimi knew very well. "I know he goes away a lot. But if he got all red and choke-y when he *did* come home, it wouldn't be fair, would it?"

"Okay," Mimi sighed. "We can't have a cat."

"That's my girl. Be good, both of you," her mother said, giving them each another kiss. "I'll be back as soon as I can."

But later, when Mimi was telling Paulette about the kitten, she still hadn't given up the idea.

"We could keep her in the garage," Mimi said. "And I would visit her every day, and play with her. We could train her to ride on Chose's back."

Mimi and Paulette were in the Nadeau backyard, sitting under a crabapple tree and watching Kenny ride around on the back of Paulette's dog. Every so often, the dog would run a short way, chasing dandelion fluff or a flying ladybug. Then Kenny would fall off, laughing in the grass.

The dog's name was Chose, the French word for "thing." Chose was a big, woolly, happy, grey-

and-white dog that was part sheepdog, part
Labrador and maybe part St. Bernard. Paulette's
father said he was mostly bear, but nobody
believed him.

"We might be able to train the cat," Paulette
said, "but could we train Chose? He sort of likes
to chase cats."

It was true. They had seen him go bounding
after Snowflake, Mrs. Filber's white Persian,
more than once.

"Chose is curious," Mimi said. "When the cats
run away, he runs after them, that's all. If they
would stay and be friends, he wouldn't do anything, I know it."

"Maybe," said Paulette. "But first you have to
find that cat. She's probably run all the way to
Calgary by now, after the way Ricky scared her."

"Poor kitten," Mimi said seriously. "What if
she gets lost and can't find her way back here?"

"What if she gets caught by the pound?"
Paulette said. "You know they look for stray cats
now just the same as dogs."

"You're right! I forgot about that!"

"If we don't give her a home," Paulette said, "sooner or later, she'll get caught. And then she'll get Put To Sleep." The two stared at each other in horror.

"We should give her a name," Mimi said, "and then maybe she'll come back to us and be safe."

"Ginger Electric Kitten Snowcone the First," said Paulette promptly.

"That's sort of long," Mimi said. "How could I call her with a name that long?"

"But it tells you all about her," Paulette said. "Like when you describe something in a story. And no other cat in the world would have that name."

"But I want to call her Princess," Mimi said.

"Call her both. Call her *Princess* Ginger Electric Kitten Snowcone the First."

"That's even longer," Mimi said, "and she won't be a kitten forever. Besides, how can we call her the first unless we know there's going to be a second? I think her name is ... " Mimi thought for a minute. "Ginger Princess," she announced.

"All right. That's a good name, too. Ginger Princess."

"Paulette! You have to come in now." It was Lucille, Paulette's oldest sister, standing at the back door.

"Okay, I'm coming." The two girls got to their feet. "See you at school tomorrow."

"Sure. Kenny, come on. We have to go home."

For a moment Kenny looked as if he was going to stay on Chose's back. But the big dog came leaping toward them and then stopped, so that Kenny fell off at their feet.

"You can ride on Chose another time," Mimi said. "Let's go home for dinner."

"Dinner!" Kenny said. "Bye, 'Sho' !"He threw his arms around the dog's neck and squeezed hard. Then he grabbed Mimi's hand and dragged her out of the yard.

They were almost all the way home, when Mimi spotted the yellow truck cruising slowly down the street. Painted on the side were the words, "Animal Control Unit."

"Oh, no," she said to herself. "They're after the Ginger Princess already!"

3

"READY, GRAMPA!" MIMI called. She wiggled down under the covers and waited.

In a moment, Grampa Takeda appeared in the doorway of her room.

"Did someone call?" he asked.

"Yes, me," said Mimi. "I'm ready for my story."

"Ah, story, *desu-ka*?" he said, and came to sit on the side of her bed. "Which story, I wonder?" He looked around the room as if he might see a story standing in the toy basket or hiding behind the chest of drawers.

"The next one in the book, of course," Mimi said, wriggling with impatience. "*You* know!"

"From this book?" He picked up the fat storybook on Mimi's bedside table.

"Yes!"

"Are you sure?"

"Grampa! It's even marked!"

"Oh, yes," he said, "so it is."

The book was called *Fairy Stories from Every Land*. They had been reading one a night for a long time. There were hundreds of stories, from Korea and France and India and Russia and Thailand and Mexico and Afghanistan — in fact from just about everywhere in the world. Mimi had made a bookmark from pink yarn so they wouldn't lose their place, but every night, Grampa Takeda seemed to have forgotten, and she had to remind him which book and which story they were reading.

Carefully, Grampa Takeda opened the book and found the place marked with the yarn. Then a big smile spread across his face.

"The story tonight is from Japan," he said. "This is the story of Little Peach Boy." And as Mimi snuggled a little deeper into her pillow, he began to read.

Once upon a time (Grampa Takeda read), there was an old woodcutter and his wife, who lived by a little stream in the forest. They wanted very much to have a child, but one never came. So they lived alone in their little cottage, with no one to look after them as they grew old.

Then one day, when the old man was away in the forest cutting wood, the old woman went to the stream to get a kettle of water. As she bent over she saw something floating down the stream toward her. It was big and round and pink. When it got close, she saw it was a giant peach.

"Oh," said the old woman, "what a beautiful big peach. I will take it into the cottage and keep it for my husband's dinner."

But when her husband came home and she took out her knife, they heard a voice crying, "Don't cut me! Don't cut me!" To their surprise, the peach suddenly split open, and out jumped a little baby boy.

"Who are you?" asked the old woman.

"Heaven saw that you were lonely without

any children," said the little boy. "I am sent to be your son."

And so they called him Momotaro, which means Peach Boy, and raised him as their son.

"Mo-mo-ta-ro," Mimi said, trying the word out. "Momotaro."

Grampa Takeda smiled at her, and then continued.

Momotaro grew quickly into a strong, good son who helped his parents every way he could. The old man and the old woman were very happy to have a son at last. Every night when they went to bed, they gave thanks for him.

One day, when Peach Boy was about fifteen, he went to his father and said, "Father, I have heard of an island out in the sea where terrible ogres live. Everyone is afraid of the ogres, who scare people and take whatever they like."

"Yes, my son. Ogre Island is truly a terrible place."

"Then, Father, I want to go to Ogre Island and fight these cruel creatures."

So the next morning, the old man and the old

woman helped their son get ready. The woodcutter found a sword and some armour for Peach Boy, and the old woman made him a lunch of delicious millet dumplings.

"What are millet dumplings?" Mimi asked.

Grampa Takeda thought for a moment. "Like little cakes."

"Cupcakes?"

"No, more like pancakes."

"Oh. Okay."

Peach Boy said goodbye to his parents (Grampa Takeda went on) and said he would come back soon. Then he walked toward the sea.

On his way, he met a little spotted dog who was going to bite him. But Peach Boy gave him a dumpling to eat, and the dog became his friend. After the dog ate the dumpling, he agreed to go with Peach Boy and fight the ogres.

On they walked, and soon they met a monkey. The monkey wanted to fight with the dog, but Peach Boy gave him a dumpling and the monkey became their friend. After the monkey ate the dumpling, he agreed to go with Peach Boy and fight the ogres.

On they walked, and soon they met a pheasant. The pheasant started to fight with the monkey and the dog, but Peach Boy gave him a dumpling, and the pheasant became their friend, too. After the pheasant ate the dumpling, he agreed to go with Peach Boy and fight the ogres.

At last they came to the sea. In the distance they could see Ogre Island. Peach Boy built a boat, and they sailed across to the island, where they saw that the ogres had a big fort.

If Peach Boy had been on his own, it would have been very difficult for him to fight the ogres. But because of his kindness, he had friends to help him.

First the pheasant flew over the walls of the fort and pecked at the heads of the ugly ogres. While they were trying to hit the pheasant with their clubs, the monkey climbed over and opened the big gate. Then Peach Boy and the dog rushed in and attacked. The dog bit the ogres, and Peach Boy cut them with his sword.

The ogres were so surprised by the attack that they surrendered. They all bowed to Peach Boy and said they were sorry. They would never steal things or scare people again.

Then Peach Boy took all their treasure. As he went home, he gave it back to the people it belonged to. When he got home, there was still lots of treasure left, so he gave some to the dog and the monkey and the pheasant. He gave all the rest to his parents. They were very glad to have him back. They said that was the best treasure of all.

Grampa Takeda looked up and started to close the book.

"Is that all?" Mimi demanded.

"Oh, yes," Grampa Takeda said, looking in the book once more. "And they all lived happily ever after."

"You always leave that out," Mimi said comfortably, "but I always remember. Thanks, Grampa. That was a good story."

"You're welcome, Mi-chan," he said, as he bent over to tuck her in and give her a kiss.

"Good night. Have a good sleep."

But when he turned out the But when he turned out the light, Mimi didn't sleep right away. She thought about the story of little Peach Boy and ... What was it? A dog, a cat, a monkey, a ... no, wait, there was no cat in it. But there *should* be one, Mimi yawned to herself. There should be a beautiful kitten named ... Ginger Princess ...

4

THE NEXT DAY, on her way to school, Mimi looked carefully in all the good cat places, but she didn't see the Ginger Princess anywhere.

"Darn Ricky Rutledge," she said to herself. "He's just like those ogres."

She began to imagine Ginger Princess as a fine Japanese lady-cat, being chased by ugly ogres that all looked like Ricky Rutledge.

Paulette hadn't seen the cat, either, but on her way to school she had seen Tim and Ricky snooping around the back of Mr. Larsen's butcher shop.

"Cats always hang around there," she said, "and Ricky had a big sack with him."

"I know," Mimi said. "I saw it yesterday."

31

"And I saw something else," Paulette said. "I saw Mr. Barchester putting something up on the bulletin board. You have to come look."

Paulette dragged Mimi to the bulletin board outside the school office. She pointed to a glossy poster. Across the top in big letters it said, "Junior Science Fair. Kids, enter your experiment in the Junior Science Fair! First Prize, $100."

While Mimi was reading the poster, a loud voice behind her said, "One hundred dollars! I can't wait!"

It was Ricky Rutledge. Tim was with him. Mimi and Paulette edged to one side, while the two boys stared at the poster.

"We've got the prize locked up, Tim," Ricky said. "Nobody's going to beat our experiment."

"You bet. Rick," Tim said. "We're real high flyers." And he nodded mysteriously.

Just then, Tanya Zagreus stopped to look at the poster. Tanya was one of the smartest kids in Mimi and Paulette's class, but she was small for her age.

"Hey, a science fair," she said. "I should think up an experiment."

"Forget it, twerp," Ricky said. "You *are* an experiment!"

Tanya looked at Ricky and Tim for a moment, and then continued to study the poster.

"Maybe something like the effects of dilute acid irrigation on bean seedlings," she said to no one in particular.

"Hey," Ricky said. "I told you to forget it. Tim and me already got it sewed up." And he grabbed Tanya's arm and twisted it.

"Ow! Let go!"

"Ow," Ricky mimicked, "Let go. Don't hurt me. You might pull my arm off."

Ricky shoved Tanya away. Then he grabbed the fat book she was carrying and slid it down the hallway like a high-speed curling rock. It reached the corner just as little Martin Pike from grade one got there. The book knocked him over like a bowling pin. Martin began to cry.

"Hey, that's a library book!" protested Tanya.

"Then you better go get it," sneered Ricky. "Real careless of you to leave it lying around where someone can trip over it."

"Yeah," Tim added, "and even more careless of you to think about entering the Science Fair."

"I can so!" Tanya said as she retreated down the hallway. "Anyone can. It says so in the rules!"

"We make the rules, kid," Ricky said. "And don't forget it."

"They're mean," Paulette said as she and Mimi walked to their classroom. "I ought to get my brother Claude after them." Claude was on his high school's wrestling team. "He would straighten them out. I wonder what their experiment is going to be?"

"I don't know," Mimi said, "but I bet it's mean. I bet you anything it's doing something awful to the Ginger Princess. But they have to catch her first."

5

MIMI WAS ON her way home that afternoon when she saw the Ginger Princess again.

There was a shortcut that Mimi usually took around the side of Forman's Shop-Rite grocery store. On one side was the rough wall of the grocery store, where you could sometimes pull off loose bits of green and blue glass. On the other side was a tall board fence leaning this way and that under the leafy branches of a tree behind the Patricia Manor apartment building.

As Mimi turned into the shortcut, she saw something move under the branches. Then the Ginger Princess walked into view along the top of the fence.

Mimi gasped. It was as if the young cat had been waiting for her. Now she walked carefully toward Mimi, looking down with interest. About a metre away, the Ginger Princess stopped and stared at her.

Mimi stared back. "Hello. Your name is Ginger Princess. Did you know that?" she said quietly. Then she made her cat-calling noise. *Psss-pss-pss-pss.* At the sound of it, the cat's head came up and her ears twitched forward. Mimi made the noise again. "Come here," she said.

Ginger Princess took a few steps forward. She peered down, looking for a way to jump from the fence. Mimi understood immediately.

"It's too high to jump," she said. "I'll catch you." And she stretched her arms up toward the cat. Her hands didn't come near the top of the fence, but it was enough for the cat. With a quick spring, she jumped, and landed with a solid thump, not in Mimi's hands but on her shoulder.

The cat began to rub against her face and purr. The noise was like a furry motor, as the cat pushed her warm, whiskery face against Mimi's.

Carefully, so as not to knock her off, Mimi raised her hands and began to pet the cat. The purring got louder.

"Oh, you darling," Mimi said. "You darling Ginger Princess. I have to take you home. Daddy won't mind if I keep you in the garage, I know it." And very carefully, she began to walk toward the end of the shortcut.

Suddenly a dark shape stepped into the passage, blocking her way. It was Ricky Rutledge. He was carrying the mail bag

"Well," Ricky said, grinning unpleasantly, "seems like you caught my experiment for me. That's real nice. Now, hand her over."

"This isn't your experiment, I mean, your cat," Mimi said. "She's mine!"

"She is not. She's a stray. And we've been chasing her for two days. So if you don't want to get hurt, just put her right in here." He held open the mouth of the mail bag.

Grabbing the startled cat from her shoulder, Mimi yelled, "Run, Ginger, run!" Then she turned and sent the cat skittering in the other direction. "Wow!" she screamed, "Wow!" hoping to make the cat run faster.

The cat ran, all right, but Mimi hadn't counted on Tim. He was standing at the other end of the narrow passage, holding an old bedspread. The cat shot toward him, aiming for the bit of daylight between his legs and the fence, but when she got close enough, Tim simply threw the ragged bedspread over her. Then he quickly scooped up the soft, struggling bundle.

"We got her, Ricky!" he called.

"Great work, Tim," Ricky said, pushing roughly past Mimi. "Just put her in here." And he held out the big bag.

"No!" Mimi screamed. "Let her go!"

"Get lost, kid," Ricky said, as Tim dropped the loudly complaining cat into the bag. "I told you, she's a stray. No one is going to miss her."

"I will! I'll miss her!" Mimi yelled.

"Gee," Tim said, "that's too bad, because she's going on a long, long trip." And they both laughed as they walked away. Ricky was carrying the bag over his shoulder. Mimi could see it moving as the Ginger Princess struggled and wailed inside.

Mimi wouldn't let Ricky and Tim hear her crying, but she couldn't stop the tears. They ran down her face all the way home.

6

MIMI WALKED INTO the backyard just as Grampa Takeda was coming out of the house. He was carrying a basket of fruit and a tea pot. Mr. Uemura was sitting in a lawn chair in the shade of the plum tree. It was a warm day, but he was wearing a cardigan sweater. His hands were folded neatly in his lap.

"Mi-chan," Grampa Takeda said when he saw her. "Come here."

"Grampa," Mimi started, "Ricky Rutledge and Ti — "

"Shh," Grampa Takeda said. "Not so loud." He looked at her. "You've been crying? Did you get hurt?"

"No, I didn't get hurt. But — "

"Then you can tell me later." He bent over and spoke quietly in her ear. "I'm very worried. Mr. Uemura is so unhappy, he has stopped eating. I just found out he hasn't eaten for the last two days. You go inside and play quietly with Kenny. I want to serve him some fruit. Maybe he will eat that."

"But, Grampa, they took the — "

"Not now, Mi-chan. Please. Go and take care of Kenny."

Grampa Takeda gently pushed her inside the house. Then he closed the door. Through the glass, Mimi saw him put the fruit and the tea pot on the little garden table beside Mr. Uemura's chair. Mr. Uemura bowed a small bow to Grampa Takeda, bending forward a little from the waist. His hands didn't reach for the fruit, though. They stayed folded in his lap.

Kenny was in the TV room, trying to cut the leg off the coffee table with his toy saw.

"Fix ca'," he said when he saw her.

He dropped the saw, picked up his toy hammer and began to hit the table.

41

"It isn't a car, it's a table," Mimi said as she flopped onto the couch.

She was too sad about the Ginger Princess to play pretend with Kenny.

"Ca'," Kenny said stubbornly. "Fix my ca'!" And he hammered even harder on the table.

"Okay, car," Mimi said. "Have it your way. Who cares, anyway?"

Just then, the doorbell rang. It was Paulette.

"Can you come out?" she asked.

Mimi looked across at her grandfather and Mr. Uemura sitting under the plum tree. Her grandfather was talking quietly, but Mr. Uemura wasn't doing anything.

"I don't think so," she said. "Want to come in?"

"Sure," Paulette said. "What's wrong?"

"Why?"

"Because you look like someone died, that's why."

"Someone probably did, or will."

Mimi told Paulette about the Ginger Princess being captured.

"That's terrible!" Paulette said.

"What are we going to do?"

"What can we do? Ricky's a big kid, and he's mean, too!"

"But we can't just let them take her like that! She's your friend! You said she was waiting for you."

Mimi thought again of the cat walking toward her along the top of the board fence. Then she remembered the whiskery face pushing against her own. "You're right!" she said firmly. "Come on. We'll go over there and spy on them right now!"

"I thought you said you can't go out."

"Actually, I don't think Grampa will notice. He's really worried right now. Only," she glanced toward the TV room, "we'll have to take Kenny, too."

"Oh, great," Paulette said. "Perfect spy team. They'll never notice us."

"I can't help it," Mimi said. "I have to look after him. But we can hide in the Neilsen place. Let's go."

The Neilsen place was next door to the Rutledge house. Mimi knew it would be all right to spy from there, because Mr. and Mrs. Neilsen were almost never home.

Since Mr. Neilsen had retired from the hardware business, they spent their winters in Mexico. In the summers, when they were back in Canada, they drove around the countryside in their mobile home, looking at irrigation dams. They went to irrigation dams because Mrs. Neilsen liked to watch birds. There were always plenty of birds around the water. But Mr. Neilsen just liked dams.

Quietly, Mimi peeked around the corner of the Neilsens' garage. The yard was empty, and the grass looked like it hadn't been cut in about two weeks. Along the far side of it ran a white board fence that was almost completely buried under a tall caragana hedge.

"It's okay," she said in a low voice. "Come on."

A moment later, Mimi, Paulette and Kenny were crouched in the shadows by the fence. They could hear voices in Ricky's yard.

"I told ya it wouldn't work like that," said one voice.

"Ya gotta tie it underneath." Mimi looked at Paulette. It was Ricky. From the sound of it, he was just on the other side of the hedge.

"I can't tie it underneath" said Tim's voice. "It isn't long enough."

Mimi bent down and peered between the boards of the fence, but the hedge was so thick that she couldn't see anything. Farther along, Paulette peered through and shook her head in frustration. She couldn't see, either.

Ricky and Tim were still talking.

"Ya have to make it longer," Ricky said. "If we don't tie it right, the cat will get out."

"Once she sees where she is," Tim said, "she won't want to go anywhere!"

"Is there enough oxygen at ten thousand metres?" Tim said doubtfully. "What if it kills the cat?"

"Then we take a picture of the body," Ricky said. "That's science, isn't it?"

Mimi shot a look of alarm at Paulette. As quietly as she could, she began to climb the fence. She had to see what was going on. It sounded like

Ricky and Tim were going to do something really awful to the Ginger Princess.

But just as she was about to swing her leg over the top board of the fence, she noticed that she was not alone. Kenny was climbing the fence with her. He grinned at her.

"Kenny!" she whispered. "Get down. You stay with Paulette." She pushed him, but he didn't move.

Paulette came up behind him and tried to lift him off the fence.

Kenny's grin disappeared. "No!" he said loudly.

"What's that?" said Ricky.

"Shh," said Mimi. "You stay with Paulette, Kenny. I'll be right back."

"No!" He started to climb even higher.

"Sounds like somebody in the next yard," Tim said.

"I bet it's someone trying to steal our experiment," Ricky said, and the hedge began to move.

Mimi jumped down from the fence. She grabbed Kenny by one arm. Paulette grabbed him by the other. Together they pulled him off the fence and galloped across the yard, dragging him behind them. They made it around the corner of the garage just before Ricky's head popped through the greenery.

"Hide in here," Paulette whispered, opening the garage door.

"They might come after us."

In a second, they were hidden behind some boxes in the cool dusty garage. Outside, they could hear Tim and Ricky looking around. "Yeah, there was someone here, all right," Ricky said. "Look at how the grass is all beaten down."

"Think they're still around?"

"Nah. They're gone. But we're going to have to be extra careful. Have to keep a real sharp look out from now on."

A few minutes later, Paulette said,"I think it's okay now. But, Mimi, what are we going to do?"

"Well," said Mimi, standing up and brushing the dirt off her knees, "the first thing to do is get Chose and bring him back here."

"You want me to go get Chose?" Paulette said, surprised.

"Yes," Mimi said. "I've got an idea. And Chose is part of it."

7

A LITTLE WHILE later, Paulette stood in front of
Mimi, trying to cover a laugh with a stern face.

"Good luck," she said, as she put Chose's leash
in Mimi's hand.

"Thanks," Mimi said, and then said it again in
her old lady voice. "Thank you very much, little
girl."

The idea had come to her while she was hiding
in the garage. She had seen an old coat hanging
there that belonged to Mrs. Neilsen. Why not dis-
guise herself? It turned out that the coat had no
buttons, but Mimi found a belt she could use to
hold it closed. The belt was a souvenir one that
said, "Lake Louise, Alberta" in black-and-white

beadwork. She also found a pair of Mrs. Neilsen's dark glasses on a shelf, with fake-diamond butterfly frames and an old floppy straw hat that Mr. Neilsen used for gardening. Wearing these, she was sure she was unrecognizable.

Disguising Chose was more of a problem. Ricky and Tim were sure to know him, even if they didn't spot Mimi.

"We could put something on his coat, to change the colour," suggested Paulette.

"Like what?"

"Well ... paint?"

"It would never come out," Mimi said, "and it might not be good for him."

In the end, they found a red bandanna, which they used to tie the woolly mop of hair on his head into a topknot. "Now he looks like a poodle," Paulette said.

"His head does," Mimi agreed.

"But what about the rest of him?"

"We can just cover him up," Paulette decided, and she threw a ragged old afghan over him and tied it under his chin. The afghan covered Chose almost to the ground on all sides.

"He looks like a sofa," Paulette giggled.

"Just as long as he doesn't look like Chose," Mimi said. "That's all that matters."

Now Mimi was ready. With Chose as her seeing eye poodle, and the taped-up handle of a hockey stick as a white cane, she was sure she looked like a little old blind lady searching for her cat. She had worried that Kenny would want to ride on the dog, but he was happy for the moment, blowing ants off the sidewalk with a bicycle pump.

"Come on, doggy," she said in her old lady voice. "Let's go find kitty."

It was hard to walk in the coat, which was so long it sometimes tripped her. The coat was hot, too. The hardest part, though, was making Chose go where she wanted. He just wanted to stop and snuffle at interesting tufts of grass, or run in a completely different direction. Mimi had to work to keep him under control. She worried that she didn't look much like an old lady when she was yanking on Chose's leash.

"Here, kitty, kitty, kitty!" Tapping in front of her with the hockey stick, she turned up the Rutledges' front walk. "Here, kitty!" She followed the walk around the side of the house, still calling.

When she got to the backyard, she saw Ricky and Tim bent over something in one corner. They stood up and stared in amazement when Mimi appeared.

"Here kitty, kitty, kitty!" Mimi said, looking around as blindly as she could. The truth was, she really couldn't see very well through the sunglasses. "What the — ?" muttered Ricky. "Am I seeing things?"

Tapping around in front of her, Mimi dragged Chose one way and then another, slowly getting closer to the two boys. So far, she didn't see any sign of the Ginger Princess.

"I don't know," Tim said. "I see it, too."

"But what is it?" Ricky demanded.

"Is someone there?" Mimi said. "Have you seen my kitty?"

She was close enough to Tim and Ricky now to see that they had been doing something to a laundry basket. But the basket was empty. The Ginger Princess wasn't there. Behind the basket, there was a tall metal cylinder, like the kind she had seen Koko the Clown using at the fair to fill balloons. On a table beside the cylinder was a gleaming yellow and red model airplane. But there was no sign of a cat.

"Say," Ricky said, "who are you, anyway?"

"I ... I'm an old lady who just moved in down the block," Mimi said in her old, cracked voice, "and I'm looking for my little kitty-cat. Have you seen her?" Just then. Chose gave a mighty lunge, almost pulling her off her feet. He seemed very interested in something behind the metal cylinder.

"Hey, get him away from there!" yelled Ricky. "That's a valuable laboratory animal."

Mimi now saw that Chose was snuffling around a wooden box that was sitting in the grass. The box had holes drilled in it. It was chained to a tree and locked tight with a big padlock. From inside the box came a low, moaning growl that got louder the more Chose sniffed around. Tim tried to shove the dog away.

Then a small, furry paw with needle-sharp claws shot through one of the holes and grazed the end of Chose's nose. The dog jerked his head back in surprise. He began to bark furiously at the box.

"It's my kitty!" Mimi said. "Good doggy! You found kitty!" She jumped toward the box, tripped on her coat and went sprawling in the grass. As she struggled to her feet again, she saw that the afghan was starting to slide off Chose's back.

"You aren't any old lady," Ricky said scornfully. He reached out and jerked the hat from her head. "You're that little Kiguchi kid, and that's Chose. Get lost, will ya? Quit bothering us!"

"But that's my kitty!" wailed Mimi.

"It is not! She's a stray and we caught her. So get out of here. This isn't your yard. Beat it."

Sadly, Mimi put the dark glasses back on the shelf and hung up Mrs. Neilsen's coat. Beside her, Paulette took the bandanna and the afghan off the patient Chose, while Kenny tried to put them back on again.

"More clothes for Sho'," Kenny insisted.

"Not now. He'll get too hot and die," Paulette lied.

"It's hopeless," Mimi said. "They've got her shut up in a box with a huge lock on it. We'll never get her out of there. And she's the most beautiful cat in the world!" Tears began to run down her cheeks.

Paulette gave her a hug. "Don't ever say 'hopeless.' She's tough. Look what she did to Chose, even when she was locked up! And they have to take her out of the box for their experiment. I heard them say so. Maybe she'll get away then."

Mimi dabbed her eyes with her sleeve. "Maybe. She *is* a royal princess. But Tim and Ricky are the ogres."

"Huh?"

"Oh, it's just a story my grampa read to me." Mimi sniffed and dried her eyes. "You're right, Paulette. I won't say it's hopeless. I'll try to think of something."

Paulette made a face. "Don't take too long, then. I also heard them say they're going to do the experiment tomorrow morning."

Mimi looked at her friend in dismay. "But that's hardly any time at all."

"I know."

"Oh, how do you think in a hurry?" wailed Mimi. "Come on, Kenny, let's go home. Maybe Grampa can think of something."

But Grampa Takeda wasn't home when Mimi and Kenny got there.

"He's over at Mr. Uemura's," Mimi's mother said. "Playing shogi with him." Shogi, Mimi knew, was Japanese chess.

For a moment, Mimi forgot about the Ginger Princess. "Why doesn't Mr. Uemura want to eat anymore?"

"I guess he's too sad and lonely," her mother said. "He's been all alone since Mrs. Uemura died last year. They never had any children."

"But doesn't he get hungry?"

"He's probably too sad to really notice. Don't you remember that time you had the flu, how you didn't want to eat?"

"Don't remind me," said Mimi. She stayed in bed, hot and cold and light-headed all at once, for nearly a week.

"Well, it's probably the same. Now, you and Kenny go and wash your hands for supper. Hurry, because I have to go to the airport soon."

"With flowers?"

"Yes. These are for a big wedding in Red Deer."

"When's Daddy coming home?"

"Next week. Do you miss him?"

"Of course. Who's going to read me a story?"

"You'll have to be a big girl and read yourself a story tonight. Grampa will be back before I go, but I don't think he'll want to talk much."

"Mum? Are you sure we can't have a cat? Even if we kept it in the garage?"

Mimi's mother looked at her in surprise. "Mimi, what's got into you? I already told you it's impossible."

"But —"

"No buts, and no cats. I'm sorry, honey, but that's just the way it is. Now, please, hurry and wash. I have to make my flowers fly."

Just when it was time for bed, Mimi's mum phoned from the airport. She said there was problem with the flowers and the airline company. She told Mimi that she and Kenny should go to bed on their own.

Of course, that meant Mimi had to get Kenny to brush his teeth and put on his pyjamas. Like always, it took him about four years just to get his shoes off. Then, when she wasn't looking, he put half a tube of toothpaste on his brush.

"Quit it. You don't need that much," she told him.

"Gonna eat it," Kenny said.

"It'll make you sick. Now put it back."

"Can't," he said, grinning.

Mimi groaned. Then she took the brush and flicked most of the toothpaste off into the toilet.

"There, that's all you need. Now, hurry up and brush your teeth."

Finally, Mimi got him into bed. She made him stay there with threats.

"If you get out of bed," she told him, "ogres will bite your toes!"

"Bad ogres," Kenny said, curling up in bed. "Sho' bite ogres."

"Maybe," Mimi said, "but not tonight. Chose is at Paulette's house. And you're here. So go to sleep."

Then she got ready for bed herself. If only Chose *would* bite the ogres, she thought. But he was too friendly. He wouldn't bite anybody. Not even kitten-nappers.

Mimi lay in bed, staring sadly at the book on her bedside table. Nothing was the way it should be. The Ginger Princess, the most beautiful cat in the world, was the prisoner of horrible ogres. Her grampa was too worried about Mr. Uemura to read her a story. Her daddy was away until next week.

She pulled the book off the table and opened it. The pink wool marked the next story, but it didn't seem fair to Grampa Takeda to read a story without him. Instead, she looked back at the pictures of the Little Peach Boy story.

There was a picture of little Momotaro being hugged by his old parents. She turned back a page. There was a picture of him walking home, pulling a huge wagon full of treasure. She could see jewels and sacks full of gold coins. Across on the other page was a picture of the big battle. Momotaro and the dog and the monkey and the pheasant were attacking the ugly ogres. The ogres were yelling with surprise and pain. One ogre had his eyes crossed. That made Mimi smile a little.

Mimi turned back another page. There was a picture of Peach Boy giving a millet cake to the pheasant, making it his friend. The dog already stood beside him. The monkey was riding on its back — just like Chose and Kenny.

Mimi looked more closely at the picture. The dog did look a little like Chose. The monkey wasn't round enough to be like Kenny, but the pheasant was sort of like Paulette.

Mimi stared at the picture for a long time. Then she lay back and thought. If Paulette looked like the pheasant, and Chose was like the dog, then who was she? Little Peach Boy? But Little Peach Boy didn't stay in bed feeling sad. He found a way to beat the ogres on their own island!

Mimi swung her legs out of bed. She got dressed quickly. Then she tiptoed out of the bed-room.

At the end of the hall, she stopped and peeked in the living room. Grampa Takeda was sitting in the big chair, facing away from her. She could tell he was listening to music because the stereo was on, and the coily headphone cord was strung across the room. All she could see of Grampa Takeda, though, was his legs the big headphones clamped over top of his silvery hair, and his hands slowly beating time beside a Japanese tea cup.

Very quietly, Mimi slipped past the living room into the kitchen, and out the back door. She hoped her mother didn't come home too soon, because she would probably look in the bedroom and find Mimi gone....

8

As she hurried down the dark, empty streets toward the Rutledge place, Mimi felt that eyes were watching her from every shadow. She wasn't supposed to be out after dark. If her mum found out, she would get into real trouble. But she just couldn't sleep when the Ginger Princess was a prisoner. Little Peach Boy didn't sleep. He went out to fight the ogres.

The only problem was, she had no idea what she was going to do when she got to Ricky's house.

There was weird yellowish-pink light from the streetlights, but it was still dark. Where trees hung over the sidewalk it was even darker.

Mimi began to imagine that she saw people hiding there, watching her go by. It made her walk even faster.

Then Mimi heard something that wasn't her imagination. It was a strange squeaking sound, like a huge bat or a rat. It was coming her way.

She stopped and listened. The squeaking got closer.

She shrank into the shadows. The noise was still coming.

Then, just as she was thinking about climbing a tree to be safe, the squeaking got really loud — and went right past her. It was someone riding an old bicycle down the street.

Mimi laughed a little to herself.

"Little Peach Boy wouldn't be afraid," she told herself. "Not of a bicycle. Not of anything!" And she marched forward again.

At the end of Ricky's street there was an empty lot. The ground here was all humpy and lumpy. Parts of it were pounded hard and rutted from kids racing their bikes and digging forts. Other parts were weedy and overgrown.

Mimi had heard that there had once been an old house here — a house that some said was haunted. Mimi didn't believe in ghosts. Besides, she played here often during the day, and knew there was nothing strange about the empty lot.

She was just cutting across the lot, when one of the blacker pools of shadow made a rustling noise. Mimi stopped. The hair began to stand up along the back of her neck.

Then the shadow spoke to her.

"Hello, Mimi," it said.

Mimi peered at the darkness.

"Who ... who's there?" She tried to keep her voice steady.

"It's me" the shadow said. "Tanya."

Mimi stepped closer and saw Tanya Zagreus sitting on the ground wrapped in a blanket. She was holding a long white tube.

"Tanya," Mimi said with relief, "what are you doing here?"

"Using my telescope," she said." My parents let me come out to look at the stars when the sky is clear. What are *you* doing here?"

Mimi sank down beside her. "I don't really know," she said unhappily. "Trying to figure out something, I guess." And then she told her the story of the Ginger Princess, and Ricky and Tim's "experiment."

When she was finished, Tanya shook her head. "That doesn't sound like science to me," she said. "That sounds dumb."

"But what are they going to *do?*"

"Oh, that's obvious," Tanya said, getting to her feet. "I think. But let's go look in their yard, and then I'll know for sure."

Obediently, Mimi followed Tanya into the alley, wondering what she was talking about.

"Okay," Tanya said, when they came to the Rutledges' fence. "Help me up on the garbage can so I can see over."

In a moment, telescope to her eye, she was looking over the fence into the Rutledges' yard.

"What do you see?" demanded Mimi. "Can you see Ginger?"

"Just as I thought," said Tanya. She turned and jumped back down into the alley. "A tank of helium. A radio-controlled model airplane. A captive passenger. They're experimenting with a steerable balloon. But the passenger is a superfluous payload."

"What? What does that mean?"

Tanya blinked at her seriously. "They're going to send the cat up in a balloon that has an airplane attached to it. The airplane is radio controlled, so they can steer the balloon. But they don't need the cat. Either the system works or it doesn't. The passenger proves nothing. Bad science," she finished, shaking her head. "It would never win a prize."

Mimi let Tanya's explanation sink in. Ricky and Tim didn't even *need* the Ginger Princess for their experiment. Somehow that made the whole thing even worse.

"But what can we *do*?" she said in desperation. "We've got to save her!"

"Well ..." Tanya put her head on one side. "I can't be sure of achieving the desired result, but I can think of several ways of disrupting the experiment ..."

When Mimi got home, her heart sank at the

sight of the van in the driveway. Her mother was home!

Pulling open the back door, she tried to slip in as quietly as she could, but her mother was standing in the kitchen, taking off her coat. It looked like she had just come in herself.

"Mimi!" she said in surprise. "What are you doing out there? Why aren't you in bed?"

"I — uh, I heard something," Mimi said weakly.

"Outside, you mean?"

"Um, yes, outside —"

"Honey, if you hear something, you mustn't go out and look! Just call Grampa. Were you worried?"

"Oh, yes," Mimi said truthfully. "I was really worried."

"Well, never mind. I'm here now, so there's nothing to worry about. Scoot off to bed this minute. I'll come and tuck you in right away."

In her bedroom, as she pulled off her clothes for the second time that night, Mimi hoped that her mother was right. Maybe there *was* nothing to worry about.

At least now she had a plan, but she didn't know if it would work.

9

IT WAS EARLY Saturday morning when Mimi knocked on Paulette's back door. Paulette came to answer, still wearing her dressing gown. As she opened the door, Chose pushed his way out, sticking his wet nose on Mimi's arm as he went.

Kenny galloped down the back steps after him. "Hi, Sho'! Hi, Sho'!"

"Come on," Mimi said. "We have to go save the Ginger Princess."

Paulette was still half asleep. "Now? I'm watching cartoons."

"Shh," Mimi said. "Not so loud. If Kenny hears he's missing cartoons, he'll yell for sure. We need to be quiet — for now."

Behind Mimi, Kenny and Chose were rolling together on the grass.

"Do we have to do it right now?" Paulette demanded.

"Yes, so hurry! We don't know when they're going to start!"

The words struck a spark in Paulette. "All right," she said. "I'll be right out."

"So, what are we going to do?" Paulette demanded. She was walking with Mimi down the street to the Rutledge place. She had brought Chose with her, and Kenny was riding on him happily.

Before Mimi could answer, Tanya appeared, walking toward them. Mimi waved. "Good," she said. "She didn't forget."

"Forget what?" Paulette asked. "What's going on?"

"Tanya's going to help us," Mimi said. "We've got a sort of plan. Hi, Tanya!"

"Good morning," Tanya said, coming up to them. "Is everybody ready?"

"I'm not," Paulette declared. "I don't know

70

what's going on."

"First," Mimi said, "we have to eat these." And she showed them a tea towel-wrapped package she was carrying. Inside were five big molasses cookies.

"They were supposed to be millet dumplings," she explained, "but we didn't have any. It doesn't matter. These will do."

"Do what?" Paulette asked.

"Make us friends for ever and ever and ever."

"We're already friends."

"But this is special," Mimi said. "This will make our friendship so strong we can defeat the ogres. It's like magic."

"Then we have to sit down some place special to eat them," Paulette said. "You can't do magic when you're walking."

They sat down on a grassy place between a mountain ash tree and a lilac bush in the Neilsens' front yard. They could hear voices at Ricky's place. He and Tim were already there. Mimi felt very serious as she carefully put the cookies in the middle of their little circle.

"Don't you have to say something?" Paulette asked.

"Like what?"

"I don't know. Something important."

Mimi thought for a moment. The only important thing she could think of was the salute to the flag.

She sat up straight, and said in a serious voice, "We salute the flag, the emblem of our country, and to her we pledge our love and loyalty, and may the Ginger Princess be free, and all ogres defeated. Amen."

Then she gave each one of them a cookie. Kenny and Chose ate theirs quickly and looked around for more. Tanya ate hers carefully, holding her free hand underneath to catch crumbs. Paulette and Mimi ate theirs slowly, feeling very solemn.

Just as they were finishing, they heard Ricky call out, "Okay, Tim, she's in there. Turn on the gas!"

Immediately something began to hiss.

Paulette, Mimi and Tanya jumped to their feet.

"All right," Tanya said. "Give me a minute to

get around the back. Once I start working, you attack from the front."

"You bet!" Mimi said, and she grabbed Kenny and dumped him on Chose's back. "Hold on tight, tight, tight," she told him fiercely. "Soon, we're going to run, and you mustn't fall off."

Then, with her eyes flashing, she grabbed Chose's collar and began to walk quickly toward Ricky's backyard.

When they got to the corner of the Rutledge house, they stopped and peeked around the corner. At first Mimi didn't know what she was looking at. Then she realized that the floppy bag spread out on the grass was some kind of big balloon, just as Tanya had expected. It was attached to the laundry basket. There was a little white-and-ginger shape inside the basket, held prisoner by the wire screen tied across it.

Tim was standing with one hand on the valve of the tall metal cylinder. Already the balloon was starting to lift off the ground along one edge. Ricky was taking a picture of it with an instant camera.

"We've got to do something!" Paulette whispered to Mimi.

"We are," Mimi whispered back. "We're going to attack!"

"Then come on!"

"Not yet!" Mimi hissed in reply. "Look!

At the far end of the Rutledges' yard, they saw the top of Tanya's face appear over the fence.

"Okay, Tim," Ricky said, "you better start up the plane and put it in. I'll work the controls." Ricky put down the instant camera and picked up a small black box.

Tim went to the airplane, did something to the motor, spun the propeller, and the engine spluttered to life. "Looks good," Tim yelled above the buzz. "I'll just put it in the frame."

He picked up the airplane and headed toward the laundry basket. Mimi saw that there was a wire harness attached to the basket, so that the airplane would ride between the balloon and the basket.

Just before Tim got there, the plane's engine suddenly picked up speed.

"Hey, Ricky, cut it out, will ya? You almost made me drop it!"

"I'm not doing anything." Ricky looked at the box in his hand and wiggled a control. The engine almost died. Then it revved up to a high scream.

"Wow! What — " The plane shot out of Tim's hands, nose dived, and then pulled out so that it was flying level, clipping the tops of the grass.

"Stop it, Rick! You're going to wreck it!"

"I'm not doing it, I tell you!" Rickey frantically jiggled the controls. The plane shot up into the air, climbing almost straight up. Then it rolled over in a lazy turn and headed straight down again toward the two boys.

"Lookout!"

"Duck!"

"It's going to crash!"

The two doubled over, but the plane pulled out of its dive before it hit them. Instead it started doing figure eights above their heads, buzzing like an angry bee.

"All right! Now!" said Mimi. She grabbed Paulette's hand and dashed around the corner, screaming, "Down with ogres! To the rescue!"

"To the rescue!" yelled Paulette.

"Hooray!" yelled Kenny.

Ricky and Tim looked up as Mimi, Paulette, Chose and Kenny thundered toward them.

"Wha — oof!" said Ricky, as Paulette ran smack into him and knocked him over in the grass.

"Save the Princess!" Mimi yelled, as she tackled Tim around the knees.

"Hey, let go," he said, and fell over beside Ricky. Meanwhile the airplane continued to howl and swoop above their heads.

"You twerp! Get off me," Ricky yelled, and he pushed hard at Paulette.

"All right," she said, "I will." And she jumped off him and headed toward the laundry basket.

"Oh, no," Ricky said, "you're not getting at that cat." And he tackled Paulette in turn.

Chose, meanwhile, had stopped to investigate the basket. From inside came the hiss and warning moan of an angry cat.

Tim struggled to escape from Mimi's arms, which were locked in a circle around his legs.

Mimi squeezed her arms tighter and bit his leg hard through his jeans.

"Yeow! Quit it!"

But Mimi only bit harder.

"You kids are gonna be *real* sorry for this." Ricky said, as he struggled to contain Paulette's thrashing legs. There was a sudden flurry of movement from the basket. Chose began to bark furiously and snap at the screen.

"Get him away from there," warned Ricky. "He's going to —"

Suddenly, one corner of the screen came away in Chose's mouth. The Ginger Princess shot out of the basket, took a quick swipe at the dog's nose, dashed straight over the balloon, and streaked up into the branches of a Manitoba maple.

Angered by the pain of his second scratched nose in two days, Chose leaped after her, roaring and barking and clawing his way through the balloon to the tree. Kenny, who had been on the dog's back laughing, fell into the laundry basket and began to cry. Paulette, who was still pinned to the ground by Ricky, was yelling, "To the rescue! Down with the ogres!"

Mimi couldn't yell, because her mouth was full of Tim's leg, but she bit harder, and that made him yell. And over it all, the airplane howled. It seemed to be flying all on its own. In the middle of all the noise, Ricky's mother appeared.

"What on earth is going on?" she demanded.

There was something in her voice that made everyone stop struggling. They all stood up quietly. Tim rubbed his leg where Mimi had bit him, but he didn't say anything. Only Chose still barked, and Kenny, on his back in the laundry basket, still cried. Overhead, the airplane had started to do barrel rolls.

Mrs. Rutledge looked at the mess. "I have never heard more racket on a Saturday morning in all my life," she said. "Ricky, stop that plane this minute."

"I ... I'm not doing anything!" Ricky protested. "Look!"

He wiggled the control on the black box again. The plane's engine promptly died. Ricky and Tim watched open-mouthed as it sailed in for a bumpy crash landing on the lawn.

"I don't believe it," muttered Tim.

Ricky, looking first at the box and then at the plane, said, "This thing is crazy!"

Mrs. Rutledge had been looking at Kenny in the laundry basket.

"Just what were you going to do, Ricky? Send this little boy up in the basket?"

"No," Ricky protested, "that wasn't it. We were —"

"And just where did you get this balloon, anyway?" She looked at the tattered rubber that now was spread across the lawn. "Is this your brother's weather balloon?"

"Well ... yeah."

"And did he say you could use it? Does he know you've got it?"

"Well, sort of ... He said he'd help with our experiment for the Science Fair."

Mrs. Rutledge looked at the laundry basket. Kenny had almost stopped crying now. He was looking out at everyone. Chose was still whining and growling around the foot of the maple tree, but he wasn't barking anymore.

In the quiet, they all could hear the hiss of gas still coming out of the metal tank.

"Tim," Mrs. Rutledge said, "turn off that helium."

Tim did as he was told.

"Ricky," Mrs. Rutledge said, "I don't want to know if you asked your brother about using his balloon and his tank of helium, because you'll have to face him yourself. I want to know — were you really going to send this child up into the air?"

"No, Mum, I wasn't," Ricky protested. "It was supposed to be a stupid cat. But these kids came and wrecked everything." Ricky's face was bright red. Mimi could see that he was close to tears. "It was for the Science Fair. We *were* going to win first prize."

"But it's *my* cat," Mimi said.

"It is not! It's a stray!"

A sudden idea came to Mimi.

"So, if she's a stray, how come I can get her down out of the tree?"

"Hunh," Ricky scoffed. "Anyone can get a cat out of a tree."

"Why don't you do it, then, Ricky?" Paulette asked sweetly.

Ricky glanced up into the tree, where the Ginger Princess now perched on a branch. "She got up there by herself," Ricky said. "Let her get down by herself."

But Ricky's mother said, "Go and get the stepladder, Ricky. That's one scared cat. If Mimi can get her down, she deserves to have her, even if she is a stray."

"Paulette," Mimi said, "you have to take Chose away."

"I'll take him home and be right back," Paulette said. "I don't want to miss this." Her eyes were flashing with excitement.

Once Chose was gone, Mimi climbed up the stepladder. When she was level with the Ginger Princess, she just looked at the cat. Her eyes were still wide and wild. She didn't seem to know Mimi at first.

"Ginger," said Mimi softly, "Ginger, it's me.

Don't be afraid."

Some of the wildness went out of the cat's eyes. She looked at Mimi more carefully.

"It's me, Ginger. Don't worry. I'll take you to a safe place, away from the terrible ogres."

The cat opened her mouth and gave a pink-tongued mew. It was an I'm-not-happy-and-I-don't-want-to-be-here mew. Mimi understood it perfectly.

"Never mind," she said. "I'll get you down." And she made her cat calling noise. *Psss-pss-pss-pss*. At the sound of it, the Ginger Princess took a step toward Mimi. Then she looked at the long drop below and crouched down again.

"I can't," said her look. "It's too high. I might fall."

"Never mind," Mimi said. "I'll bring you down."

She stepped up another step on the ladder and reached for the cat. She felt hands below steady the ladder, but she didn't look down. Very gently, she lifted the Ginger Princess off the branch. The cat had her claws out because she was afraid of falling, but she didn't scratch Mimi. Instead, she hung on tight, looking wide-eyed over her shoulder as Mimi backed carefully down the ladder.

When Mimi got down on the ground, she saw that Paulette was holding the ladder. She had a big grin on her face.

"I guess she's your cat, all right," said Mrs. Rutledge. "Ricky, apologize."

"Aww, do I ..." Then he caught a look at his mother's face. "Sorry," he mumbled.

"I hope so," his mother said. "Now you and Tim can start cleaning up. And when you're finished, you can start thinking about what you're going to say to your brother when he gets home from cadets. It took him a long time to save up for the balloon and that helium, you know."

Mimi's arms were still full of the Ginger Princess. "Let's go, Paulette," she said. "Can you bring Kenny?"

10

As she walked down the street carrying the Ginger Princess, Mimi was so happy she felt like she was a balloon herself.

"Oh, you poor cat," she kept saying over and over. "You're safe now. Yes, you are."

Paulette was just as happy. "That was great!" she said. "We beat the ogres! You should have seen the way Tim went down when you tackled him."

"I did see it," Mimi said. "*You* should have seen the look on Ricky's face when you ran straight into him!"

"Sho' ran fast," said Kenny happily, "an' Mimi got a kitty." He reached for the cat's tail.

Paulette grabbed his hand. "Don't play with kitty now," she warned him. "She might scratch."

Tanya joined them at the corner. "Down with bad science!" she said with a big grin. "We won!"

"Oh, Tanya," Mimi said. "Thank you! You flew that plane just like a pilot!"

"Was that *you* flying the plane?" Paulette asked in surprise. "I thought it was Ricky."

"Oh, no," Tanya said. "The plane was answering my controls, not his. That's why he was so surprised." And she pulled another black box from her pocket.

"But," said Paulette, "how did you know the plane would listen to yours and not his?"

Tanya's grin got even bigger. "Because I sneaked in last night and took the batteries out of his!"

All three laughed so loudly that Kenny began to yell.

"Down with the ogres," Mimi crowed.

"Hooray!" yelled Kenny.

"The millet cake cookies worked! We saved the Ginger Princess. But," Paulette said, "what are you going to do with her now? I thought you couldn't have a cat because of your dad's allergies?"

"You're right," Mimi said. "We can't. But I've got another idea. Follow me."

Mimi led the way past her place, down the street and around the corner, carrying the warm weight of the Ginger Princess all the way. At last she stopped in front of a small white house with a sun porch on the front.

"Who lives here?" asked Paulette.

"You'll see." Mimi pushed through the gate, went up to the front door and knocked.

They could see someone moving, through the curtains. Then Mimi's grandfather opened the door. He looked surprised to see her.

"Mi-chan," he said, "what are you doing here?"

"Hi, Grampa. Can I see Mr. Uemura?"

She was afraid he might say no, but he just stood aside with a funny look on his face and let her come in.

"Hi, Grampa," Kenny said. "We ran fast!" And he sat down in the open doorway.

Mr. Uemura was sitting back on an old couch. A bright crocheted blanket lay across his legs. A little bit of sunlight came through the curtains and splashed across him, but he didn't look very warm. He looked old and tired and thin.

"Hi, Mr. Uemura," Mimi said.

Mr. Uemura nodded just a tiny bit, but he didn't look at her. He was looking out the window at nothing in particular.

While Paulette, Tanya and Kenny stayed by the door, Mimi went and stood in front of Mr. Uemura.

"Mr. Uemura," she said, "do you know the story of Little Peach Boy? Of Momotaro? How he saved people from the terrible ogres?"

Behind his dark glasses, Mr. Uemura's eyes were looking at Mimi now.

"We saved this kitten from some boy-ogres," Mimi said, "but she doesn't have a home. She's all alone, with no one to look after her. We can't keep her because my dad gets all red and can't breathe when there's a cat around. But I don't want to give her to the pound, because they'll just put her to sleep, and that's not fair. Do you think you could look after her?"

And before Mr. Uemura could say anything, she put the Ginger Princess in his lap.

The cat stepped from Mimi's arms onto the blanket. She stretched first one back leg and then the other. She was a little stiff from being carried so far. Then she sat down in the sunlight that was falling on Mr. Uemura's legs, and began to wash her face.

Mimi held her breath. It wasn't enough for the Ginger Princess to like Mr. Uemura. Mr. Uemura had to like the cat, too. For a moment he watched the cat making herself look clean and pretty. Then, very slowly, he lifted one hand.

"Oh, no," Mimi thought. "He's going to push her off."

But instead, Mr. Uemura's hand began, very slowly, to stroke the cat. At his first touch, she looked up as if she had heard someone call her name. Then she finished her wash by turning and licking both her sides and Mr. Uemura's hand. After that she lay down in his lap. She squinted her eyes in the sunlight. And she began to purr.

Mimi let out the breath she had been holding. She knew it was going to be all right.

That night, when Mimi got into bed, Grampa Takeda came to tuck her in.

"Mi-chan," he said, "you did a very good thing today. I think you saved Mr. Uemura's life."

"Is he going to be all right?"

"I think so. It will take time for him to get all better, but after you left, he ate *two* pieces of apple, and a cracker."

"What about the Ginger Princess?"

Grampa Takeda's eyes shone. "After a while, she got up and walked all over his house, looking here, looking there — but very lady-like, you know. I told him she might be hungry. So he sent me to the store for cat food. And after I opened the can, he fed her himself. She is happy there. When I left, she was sleeping beside him. And he couldn't stop looking at her."

"Oh, good," said Mimi. "Then that makes *two* lives I saved. If Ginger had gone up in that balloon, who knows where she would have ended up."

Grampa Takeda nodded seriously. "It wasn't a very good experiment."

"And I can visit her whenever I want?"

"Oh, yes. Mr. Uemura wants you to come every day. He says you are like the mother of the Ginger Princess."

Mimi sighed happily. "Then it's almost like having her live here with us. Grampa, can I have a story tonight?"

Grampa Takeda smiled at her. "Not tonight, Mi-chan. Tonight, I go back to see how Mr. Uemura and the cat are doing. But tomorrow — tomorrow, you get a story for sure. Maybe even two stories!"

"Okay, Grampa. Thanks."

Mimi snuggled happily into her pillow as he bent over to give her a kiss.

"Good night. Little Peach Girl," he said. "Have a good sleep."

And Mimi did.

Read more Streetlight adventures!

Seven Clues

Matt is so bored. It's summer vacation, all his friends are away, and there is nothing to do in Pebble Creek — that is, until he receives a mysterious postcard.

> There's something you should look for
> It will bring you great pleasure
> Not coins in a pirate's chest
> but a different sort of treasure

A treasure? In Pebble Creek? If Matt had something better to do, he'd throw the postcard away. But he doesn't, and one clue leads to another...

Seven Clues is the first book in Kathy Stinson's trilogy of adventure stories set in Pebble Creek. Enjoy it with *The Great Bike Race* and *One More Clue* — or each story on its own!

ISBN10 1-55028-889-X
ISBN13 978-1-55028-889-6 $8.95

The Great Bike Race

Matt leaned over his handlebars, ready for the Go. Sweat trickled down the side of his face. He reached up to wipe it away. Bang!

Can Matt win the town's bike race? He thinks so. Not only is he fast, but he really needs the first prize-an awesome new mountain bike-to replace his old clunker. But Matt's pals all think they can win, too. And practising for the race seems to bring out the worst in everyone. Pretty soon the competitors are barely speaking. Can Matt stay friends with the others after the race is over? If he loses, will he want to?

The Great Bike Race is the second book in Kathy Stinson's trilogy of adventure stories set in Pebble Creek. Enjoy it with *Seven Clues* and *One More Clue* —or each story on its own!

ISBN10 1-55028-888-1
ISBN13 978-1-55028-888-9 $8.95

One More Clue

While cleaning his neighbour's attic, Matt uncovers two mysterious items: a magician's costume and a poem written on a dusty, yellowed piece of paper.

> There's something you should look for
> Which I hope that you will treasure
> Searching for it by yourself
> Is important beyond measure.

Could it be an ancient clue for some long-ago treasure hunt? With the help of his friends, Matt sets out to discover the history of this decades-old mystery — and possibly a treasure!

One More Clue is the third book in Kathy Stinson's trilogy of adventure stories set in Pebble Creek. Enjoy it with *Seven Clues* and *The Great Bike Race* — or each story on its own!

ISBN10 1-55028-890-3
ISBN13 978-1 55028-890-2 $8.95

Runaway Gran

by Sonia Craddock

Rosy's grandmother keeps vanishing. Where does she go when she disappears? And does Gran really know, as she claims, where a secret treasure can be found? Rosy unravels these persistent puzzles in this touching, off-beat mystery about the joys and sorrows of family life.

ISBN10 1-55028-953-5
ISBN13 978-1 55028-953-4 $8.95

MEMBER OF SCABRINI GROUP

Québec, Canada
2006